CONTENTS

CHAPTER 1

A Stitch in Time

When I wake, I don't open my eyes. I know where I am. The hard, blunt sound of traffic and horns honking and people shouting feels like rocks thrown at my ears. The sound never stops, but it's even louder in the early morning.

I think back to when there was nothing in my ears but the clucks of our chickens and my parents' soft voices in the next room. Back when I was just Hanh. Hanh, the girl who went to school and dreamed about a better future.

Now I feel as hard and heavy as the wooden floor beneath me. I wish I had my sleeping mat, but it's back home. I remember helping to make it. I picture Ma working in our field, cutting and splitting the reeds for the mats and then drying them in the sun.

I think of how I helped to dye the reeds green, red and yellow in the cook pot with my older sisters. *"Hanh, you're spilling water everywhere!"* my sisters would say. The four of us laughed around the giant pot until Dad came in and told us off and we all took the coloured reeds outside to dry.

When the reeds were ready, Ma and Grandma would weave them into mats at the loom. They worked so fast, like two parts of the same happy machine. Ma and Grandma didn't speak much, but they smiled a lot.

My reed sleeping mat is so far away, but when I close my eyes, the smiles of my family feel closer.

A knee pushes against my ribs. I know it's only Ping, one of the eleven other girls in here. We go to sleep lined up on the floorboards like matches in a box. But most nights Ping twists round in her sleep till she's lying nearly sideways.

The other girls hate the way she does that. They used to pinch her to wake her up. Ping would pinch them back and then everyone would be shouting and we'd all be up. So I put up with Ping's knee in my ribs and we all sleep a bit longer.

The early-morning sun shines into dirty windows that are nailed down. Another day is beginning. Are my family out there somewhere looking for me? Will I ever be found?

"Hanh," Ping whispers to me. "Hanh, you crying again?"

"No way," I hiss.

Ping sighs. "Nor me," she says, and wipes her cheek.

Then I hear the rattle of keys, same as every morning. The door shakes as the big lock turns. The door is thrown open. Our

supervisor fills the doorway. Her name is Yen. She doesn't look that mean, but she is. She has the big stick she always carries in her hand and a sneer on her face. The girls start to stretch and struggle up from the floor.

"Come on, pigs. Up!" Yen shouts at us. "Want your morning meal? Work for it. Another shipment came in last night. It needs turning round today."

Yen decides that Ping is too slow. She steps forward and kicks Ping in the leg. Ping winces, but she says nothing. None of us do. Yen will do worse if we say anything.

I lead the way out of the room and into the dingy corridor. The windows are boarded up so we can't see out and no one can see in. I give a longing look to the small bathroom as we pass it. No one's allowed to use it till we've worked at least two hours. We're only allowed eight minutes in the bathroom twice a day, so each trip needs to count.

We trudge down the stairs towards the Room. It's so noisy, we can hear it from down the hallway. The giant machines growl and blast, vibrating the door. The steaming hiss of the clothes presses sounds like a giant serpent. Male voices shout to each other over the chattering noise of metal needles punching into cloth.

Tuyet, my friend, has a coughing fit behind me. Tuyet coughs a lot these days. She had asthma before she got here and now it's worse. She's thirteen, just a few months older than me. Yen calls me and Tuyet "the babies" cos she's seventeen. Most of the others are fifteen.

"I can't go in, Hanh," Tuyet whispers. "My chest is so tight and I'm last for the bathroom today. I can't."

"You can," I say. "You can do this." It's like I'm telling myself too.

My eye is drawn to some graffiti carved into the wall above the door to the Room. It reads: *One way in, no way out.* I wonder who wrote it. How long they were in this place.

What happened to them.

But I can't give up. That's just not me. I take Tuyet's hand and I squeeze her fingers. "You can have my bathroom slot," I whisper. "I'm second up."

"I can't do that to you, Hanh," Tuyet says. "It's not fair."

"I'll take it," says Ping behind us.

Tuyet raises a fist to her and says, "You'll take this, snoop!"

Ping retreats and Tuyet follows, still coughing. Yen tells them both to shut up. But Tuyet seems determined to say something to Ping – it'll be nothing good, I'm guessing.

Well, whatever. I know Tuyet *will* take my bathroom spot. But I also know she'll give me a mouthful of her rice later to say thank you. Friends help each other. Besides, my name means "right behaviour" and Ma always wants me to live up to it.

I try. I do try. *Think positive*, I tell myself, over and over. If I keep going, the day will pass, minute by minute, until it's finally over. Then the day will drag itself off into the dark, same as the rest of us.

The Room is where I work, with the other boys and girls here. We make jeans and jackets. We cut, sand, embroider, press and distress the denim, working till our fingers bleed. For twelve hours each day, we turn out cheap fast fashion: clothes that will wear out as fast as we do.

Yen says the things we make are sold all over the world. Piled high in big, bright clothes stores. Made by us. Bought by people like you.

This place is our whole world, far away from yours.

And this is my story. I'm going to tell it to you.

CHAPTER 2

The Room

Yen turns the heavy handle and opens the door to the Room. Time to go inside.

Into the sweatshop.

The first few times you enter, your senses just want to hide away. The Room attacks all the senses, with noise and heat and the stink. The stink from the chemicals in the dye station in the corner strips the back of your throat.

The dye station is where they bleach jeans and denim jackets. Sometimes all over;

sometimes just in patches. There's a drain in the corner where the bleach is meant to go, but it needs unblocking. We end up working beside a pool of chemicals. It doesn't help the headaches.

Anyway, the bleaching doesn't happen until the jeans are made to look pre-worn – you know, the way they have holes in, or frayed pockets, or faded patches? Well, they're not really "worn" by anyone. We just make them look that way.

Along the far end of the Room there are these plastic legs dangling from the ceiling. You push the jeans over them and hit a button so the legs inflate. That makes the denim smooth so you can blast it with sand from a high-pressure gun. The sand comes out so fast it looks like water, and it scuffs the material. *Abrading* it, Yen says. She's been taught the word and she shows it off. Once the denim is abraded, it's softer and nicer to wear for the lucky customer.

There are fans at the back of the Room. They're meant to suck the grains of sand and the tiny bits of blasted denim from the air. But the fans turn so slowly it's like they've given up.

Sometimes shafts of sunlight make it past the dirt on the high windows and you can see the dust dancing like a thick swarm of flies. The dust-flies look alive. They fill the Room. They fill our lungs. We have to swallow them down till we choke. Like I said, Tuyet coughs most of the time. It's just one more noise in the Room.

We had masks at the start. Yen's bosses took them away because they needed them for an inspection at another factory. They wanted the inspector to think things were OK for the people who work there. We didn't get the masks back. But I hope the people who wear

them now are feeling better. You don't know –
things might be even worse at that factory
than here.

Tuyet takes her place at the large steam
presses closest to the sandblast area. She pulls
clothes from a mountain of jeans beside her
and begins to arrange them on the press. The
steam will bake in the creases around the front
of the thighs for a more vintage look.

We must make hundreds of jeans and
jackets each day. When they're done, it's
Chau's job to fix on the tags and labels. Chau
is beautiful, with her big eyes and timid smile.
But she also gets distracted – especially by the
thought of food. Some of the clothes need to
be put on hangers, some sealed into plastic
bags. Chau gets mixed up sometimes and then
Yen kicks her. I tried to stick up for Chau once
and Yen slapped me so hard my teeth hurt for
two days.

I guess we are like the jeans – roughed up by hand when we have to be.

Ping is fifteen years old, small, dark and quiet. She runs small electric sanders over the seams and hems and the pocket edges. It's called "distressing the detail". When the tools break down, she has to distress the denim by hand. Different sandpapers give different effects, but they all leave Ping's fingers raw.

It's crazy. The denim starts off so perfectly blue, like new. Then we wreck it. People pay extra for someone to ruin their clothes before they're even worn! How did that ever become a thing?

Well, in any case, I know I'm lucky. I don't have to distress or abrade or dye or blast anything. I take my place at my dusty workbench at the back of the Room and the sewing machine's red power light glares at me. I press the pedal with my bare foot to turn the light green – and I wait to be given that sign to

14

GO. Then I'll be embroidering designs all the way up to the knees of these roughed-up jeans. From the length of them, these must be jeans for girls my own age.

At the next desk, Kim-Ly folds herself into her chair and picks up her needle and thread ready to sew tiny beads and buttons onto my design. These are called "accents" – they give the flowers depth and texture.

Kim-Ly is tall and thin as a bundle of reeds and she grinds her teeth as she works. It's the tiniest noise, but sometimes it seems so loud. Especially at night.

Tuyet hates it. This one time while we were working, Yen hit Kim-Ly in the face with her stick. I looked away and saw Tuyet praying: *"Please let Kim-Ly's teeth be knocked out, please, please, please."* I was so shocked I laughed out loud and Kim-Ly thought I was laughing cos she was hurt. She didn't speak to me for a week.

Kim-Ly isn't the only one who's given me the silent treatment. Some of the girls are jealous of those of us who do the sewing. They think we have it easy, so they give us dirty looks.

I can understand why, I guess. We're furthest from the dye station and the sandblast area, and Yen doesn't shout at us so much because we manage to keep up with the quotas. Most of the time anyway.

But we're not suck-ups. We're good with needles and thread, that's all. I never used a sewing machine before I got here, but I did a lot of sewing by hand at home and I learn fast.

I used to help Ma repair clothes at the market. The clothes came from all over. I dreamed of becoming a fashion designer, making all my own clothes. I would sit and mend and sew and listen in to Ma and her friends as they shared news and gossip and secrets.

They would forget about me, working in silence, so they didn't guard their words. I loved their stories. Stories about visiting big cities or even travelling to other countries. At night, before I slept, I played out their stories in my head. Sometimes I imagined that I was taking part in those stories myself. That was where I wanted to be when I was older – not telling tales with women in the marketplace but out in the world living them! Then they could talk to each other about *me* exploring far from home. The thought of that made me dizzy.

That's why I was so thrilled to go to school. I knew my family could hardly afford the books and pens and supplies I needed. But I wanted to learn. I didn't care that I had to walk three kilometres to reach school, over the hills and across the steaming grass as the sun rose, and three kilometres back home again. Each time I walked home it was like my head was in the clouds as I dreamed about my glittering career as an international fashion designer ...

Suddenly there's a clatter and a shriek in the Room.

Tuyet.

I look up to find Tuyet has left her steam press and crashed into Ping at the sanding desk. Tuyet gets up from the floor gripping her hand, which is covered in blood. Ping holds her sanding tool, which is bloodied too. It's still whirring.

"You useless pig!" Yen yells. She thunders up to Tuyet and shoves her backwards. "Don't get blood on the denim or the bosses will kill us all. What did you do?"

Tuyet's panting, like she wants to scream, but she starts a coughing fit instead.

Ping turns off her sander. "I didn't do anything," she says. "I was working with the sander, and Tuyet grabbed it as she fell."

"I burned my wrist on the press," Tuyet says, her voice raspy. "I jumped back and knocked into Ping. Look, I'm hurt!" Tuyet sticks out her wounded hand and blood bubbles from it. Ping groans and looks like she's going to be sick.

"Please, Yen, I need stitches," Tuyet begs. "I need a doctor."

"You'll need an undertaker if we don't meet quota," Yen replies. With a growl, she shoves

Tuyet towards a tall boy who's just finished his shift on the sandblaster. "Take this clumsy fool to the office. See what they say."

Yen kicks the clothes press and glares round at us all. "If we fall behind, I get it in the neck," Yen says. "And if that happens ..." She mimes a knife across her throat with her finger. "I'll take it out on *yours*."

Yen's threat hangs around like one more bad smell in the Room. I look away and see Tuyet's face as she's led away clutching her hand. But get this: she's smirking. As for Ping, she's watching the door as it closes and there's the hint of a smile on her face. I remember how Tuyet went after Ping just before we came into the Room earlier. How they spoke to each other.

What's going on?

There's no way to know. I just hope Tuyet's OK.

She won't be using my bathroom break after all, I guess.

*

Tuyet doesn't come back all morning. She even misses breakfast at ten o'clock. Chau almost starts a fight by trying to claim Tuyet's portion of rice and vegetables for herself. I calm things down by letting Chau eat mine. All I have in my belly is a ball of worry. If Tuyet's hand is messed up, she won't be able to work the press. What will the factory owners do with her?

A worrying idea has stuck in my mind. While we can work, we're safe. But when we can't …

What then?

CHAPTER 3

The Fall from Heaven

I try not to worry about Tuyet as I embroider lines of coloured thread into blooming flowers on happy waving stems. I copy the same pattern exactly, again and again and again. It's kind of hypnotic. I can lose myself in it and almost forget the hunger, the thirst, the stink and the bad taste in my mouth.

I daydream about how I used to walk home from school, thinking about everything I'd learned. I was sure that if I studied super-hard,

I could find a good job in fashion one day and help my family.

That day arrived sooner than I ever thought it would.

The day that *they* came – the Man and the Woman from the city.

They were like no one I had seen before in our district. I'd just walked back from school and I found them in the house waiting for me.

Like dogs waiting for food.

The Man wore a smart suit that was cool grey like the clouds on a rainy day. He wore a strong fragrance. It seemed to fill our small home.

The Woman's dress was greener than our rice fields and she wore a delicate hat on her waves of black hair. Ma couldn't take her eyes from it. She only owned a cone-shaped hat to protect her from the sun and the rain. Ma stared at the Woman's hair and make-up like she was in a trance.

"You are welcome here," my dad said. "But why have you come?"

The Man smiled at me. "Because of your daughter," he said.

The Man and the Woman said they both worked for a fashion company that was opening a new shop in Hanoi, 200 kilometres away. They wanted young girls to work there as shop assistants. Training would be given. Wages would be paid.

I couldn't believe it. This could really help me build a future and help support my family! But why me?

"I have family in Bac Kan Province," the Woman said. "I understand your cousin lives there?"

Dad beamed, astounded. "How could you know that?"

"Your cousin suggested I come here!" the Woman revealed. "His neighbour's daughter, Tuyet, is going to join us too."

I had met Tuyet before. I thought she seemed nice.

The Woman smiled at me and said, "If you work for us for a year, we will give your parents three million dong."

(Does that sound a lot to you, where you live? Well, it is. It's about £100 in your money. Riches.)

My family couldn't believe the Man and the Woman were offering so much. The money I'd earn would make our farm work much better. We could afford to dig channels in the soil to bring water to the whole rice field. We could buy animals. Maybe get a generator so we had electricity all the time. And if Ma didn't have to work so much, she could take better care of Grandma.

But what about me? Things were happening so fast. I was scared to say it, but I had to ask: "What about school?"

Dad looked angry. "You can catch up on school when you get back, if you want," he said.

There were tears in Ma's eyes. I knew how much it meant to her for me to go to school. "It's only for a year," Ma muttered.

The Woman nodded eagerly.

I thought about it. There was a girl in my class who was two years older than the rest of us. Girls her own age teased her about being behind. But maybe I could find a way to learn while I was away in Hanoi so I didn't fall so far behind?

The Man said that if my parents signed a form to say I could work for them, they would give them some money right now and more would be sent to them each month.

"You need to decide soon, or it will be too late," the Woman said. "The coach leaves for Hanoi from Bac Kan in three days. It is almost full already because so many girls want to go." She looked at me and smiled, nodding. It was like she was looking at an angel, not at me. "There are so many good and sensible girls that want the best for their families and for themselves," the Woman added.

I looked down politely. She was right – I should put my family first.

The Man reached into his jacket pocket for a wad of banknotes. He peeled off two notes – one pink, one yellowish green – and held them out to my dad.

Dad hesitated. I met his look. His eyes were reaching for me, but his shaking hands were reaching for the notes.

The Man lowered his hand. Dad's fingers closed instead on a piece of paper held out by the Woman.

"This is a contract," she told him. "Terms of your daughter's employment. You will want to read it. Check everything is in order."

My dad turned his eyes to the words on the paper. But he cannot read. He never went to school. No one in my family can read at all apart from me. The contract might have said anything. I wanted to see, but I couldn't shame my father in front of *them* by showing he couldn't read.

My mother went to the altar in the hall and said she would ask our ancestors for their blessing. They must have given it fast because Dad signed the contract. The Woman smiled and the Man handed him the two banknotes.

Where you live, it would buy you maybe two cups of coffee.

That day, it was enough to buy me.

*

Two days later, I hugged my dad and my sisters goodbye. The minibus to Hanoi was leaving at 4 p.m. from the bus station in Bac Kan near the market.

Ma went with me to the bus station in the back of a neighbour's car. The car didn't break down for once, so we arrived an hour early. Ma and I sat on red plastic chairs under a faded canopy that flapped over us weakly, like a broken wing. For a treat, Ma used some of the money we'd been given to buy us tea. I smiled and pretended I liked the taste. For the first time, we couldn't think of much to talk about.

Then Tuyet appeared and she was so excited it made me feel warmer inside. We chatted and then more girls arrived. Some of them were Tày people, dressed in beautiful indigo blue. They didn't speak our language, but all twelve of us wore the same smiles.

We didn't know when we would be back, but Ma was sure the Woman and the Man would arrange visits for holidays like Lunar New Year and Liberation Day. I began to feel I was starting out on a great adventure.

The minibus came. We loaded our little bags on board and I got butterflies. Ma tried to hug me, but I didn't want to look like a baby in front of the other girls. I sort of pulled away and gave her a brief wave as I hurried onto the minibus. I didn't look back.

Why didn't I look back? Just one more time.

We cheered as the minibus bumped and rattled away, full of nerves and bravado. The Woman sat alone at the front. She wore dark glasses and a shawl, and she never once looked at us.

Hanoi was a journey of four hours to the south, but I chatted with Tuyet and we got talking to Ping and Chau. Soon the four of us

were having a fine time. None of us had ever
been on an expressway before. There were so
many lanes, so many cars and signs. We were
driving so fast. I felt giddy, entering a different
world.

The memory reminds me now of an old
legend my grandma told me about the Nang
Tien Grotto in Luong Ha. Once upon a time
there were seven fairies that came down
from heaven to swim at the foot of Phja Trang
Mountain. The fairies had such fun together,
they did not notice when night came. And
in the dark, the fairies could not fly back to
heaven. So the Creator made the beautiful
grotto into a place they could call home, and
there the fairies stayed.

Tuyet and Ping and Chau and I were talking
so much that we didn't notice the miles passing
and night falling. But then suddenly we were
in the city. I remember feeling so scared of

the rushing traffic, the overwhelming riot of colours, sights and smells.

But we hardly had a chance to look as we were bundled off the minibus and into the factory.

And just like that, our fate was sealed. Like the fairies, there was no way back home for us now.

But this horrible factory was worlds away from a beautiful grotto. If the Creator made this place for us to live in, we must have hurt him badly in another life.

*

I'm scared it's Tuyet who's badly hurt now, because she doesn't come back to the Room all day. I keep hoping that she'll walk in. I don't even mind when they cancel our second bathroom break to make up for time we've lost, because I don't want to miss her return.

But Tuyet doesn't show, and a little after 7 p.m. Yen opens the door. "Right, you pigs," she shouts. "Noses to the trough. Go."

Work is over – now we get the second of our two meals a day.

We eat without Tuyet. Looks like she's gone.

And the ball of worry in my belly feels as hard as stone.

CHAPTER 4

Hungry Ghosts

We eat in a big room with breeze-block walls. We always have rice – sometimes with slimy vegetables, sometimes with scraps of chewy meat. But mostly rice on its own. It's the same stuff they give us at breakfast, only older and drier. There's never anything else.

We use our hands to scoop the rice from the big tray onto plates. Then we gulp it down. I sometimes feel like one of the hungry ghosts in Grandma's stories: a lost soul reborn with a mouth as small as the eye of a needle and a stomach as large as a mountain, as punishment for some evil I've long forgotten. My belly can never be filled.

I sit next to Ping. "Where's Tuyet?" I ask her.

Ping swallows her mouthful of rice and says, "How should I know?"

"I saw you and Tuyet talking," I say. "And Tuyet looked pleased when she left the Room."

"Tuyet fell on Ping on purpose," says Kim-Ly, gulping down sticky rice. "I saw it all. I saw Ping push the tool into her hand."

Ping blinks and then shrugs. "She wanted me to," Ping says. "Got her out of work for the day."

"Tuyet's hand looked bad," I say. "Maybe they took her to hospital?"

Even as I say it, I know it's wishful thinking. Doctors cost money. We don't. That's why we're here.

"Maybe they had to chop her whole hand off," Chau says from across the table. She picks some rice from her teeth. "I bet Tuyet's dead."

"Don't be stupid," Ping says. "She'll be all right."

We clear our plates away and go out into the paved courtyard where we have to exercise.

The Tày girls trudge along, talking quietly. I envy the way they stick together. I feel sad and lost without Tuyet, without that link to my home.

The sound of the city is all about us. It is a roaring urban sea with endless energy but no purpose I can understand. We can't see much of the city from down here. We're overlooked only by the Moon, hanging up there like a dim old light bulb cobwebbed by clouds.

I wonder how many weeks have gone by since we got here? The Moon helps me keep track. It was full when we arrived. Since that night it's shrunk away to nothing and grown back again three times.

That must mean we've been here for about three months.

I'm shrinking more slowly than the Moon, but I'm afraid I will never grow back. If only we could get away from here. Fly back to our homes like spirits. Escape and wake back on our sleeping mats, and blink away this nightmare.

A woman in shadow watches us from the doorway. After ten minutes of wandering, we'll have to go back inside. A shouty man used to make us do drills with footballs, but he's gone now. The footballs stayed behind, but they're really deflated. We still kick them around sometimes, when we're angry.

I see Yen at a window on the floor above. I've heard she has a room to herself there, along the landing from the male dorm. I guess she uses us the same way that we use the football – to let out her frustrations. She bosses us. She gets to beat us. But someone else gets to beat her if she doesn't make us work hard enough.

Yen moves away from the window and my gaze trails upward to the dark, dirty windows of our bedroom. If they were clean, we could look out at the city. There's not much of a view – there's only an office building across the parking lot. But it would be nice to know that life is still going on outside.

"Tuyet!"

I hear Ping's cry behind me and spin round in a heartbeat. Tuyet is standing there in the yard. I can see her clothes are covered in scraps of feathery white. She smiles as I run up to her.

I grab her hard and shout, "Tuyet! You're all right?"

"No, I'm not," Tuyet says, and just manages to stop one of her coughing fits. She holds up

her hand, covered in stained-brown bandages. "This hurts like hell and it got me nowhere." She kicks one of the old footballs into the wall, so hard it knocks dust from the brickwork.

"The bosses didn't let me rest," Tuyet says. "Never even gave me an aspirin. They took me to a different dump they own, right across the city. A cotton factory where they make shirts and tops. I was on my knees all day, groping around under the sewing machine tables picking up scraps of cotton."

"That sucks," I say. "I'm glad you're back."

"Not to stay, Hanh," Tuyet tells me. "They're gonna keep sending me there." She shudders. "Every day. Till my hand's better and I can work the press again."

Kim-Ly has trotted over. "How long will that take?" she says. "You're so selfish. With you gone, it's more work for the rest of us."

"Well, why don't *you* try wrapping your palm around a hand-sander?" Tuyet says. She squares up to Kim-Ly on her tiptoes. "Even better, try sitting on one."

Kim-Ly answers by snatching out a long, blunt needle from her waistband. She pricks the back of Tuyet's good hand. Tuyet gasps.

"If you want a hole in the other hand, just say," Kim-Ly growls.

The other girls gather round, like sharks drawn to blood.

"Stop it," I say to everyone as I knock the needle from Kim-Ly's fingers and push between her and Tuyet. "We need to stick together, not fight."

Tuyet keeps her eyes locked on Kim-Ly's for a few seconds longer. Then she looks away and nods. The crowd drifts off, disappointed.

Kim-Ly stalks away. Only Chau stays, holding her stomach and looking at Tuyet with big eyes.

"What was the food like where you went?" Chau asks.

*

At lights out, Tuyet pushes in between me and Ping on the floor. Ping protests, but Tuyet just says, "Put your knee in my ribs and I'll cough all over you."

Ping yawns and shrugs. Tuyet settles on her side. She's holding herself really still, but I can hear the wheeze in her breath. Her asthma is bugging her.

I reach out in the dark and find Tuyet's fingertips. I squeeze them. She doesn't speak. It's only from the catch in her breath that I know she's crying.

"Does your hand hurt?" I whisper, and I know it's a silly question. Of course it hurts. Everything does here. And Ma was wrong. We will never be allowed out for holidays – not for Liberation Day or New Year or even Ho Chi Minh's birthday.

Ho Chi Minh is said to have been our country's greatest leader. We called him Uncle Ho in school. He was kept in a prison in China because they thought he was a spy. He wrote poems there and we learned one in school. It was about how the words for dragon and prison look fairly similar in the Chinese picture language. I remember one line that said: "*When the prison doors are opened, the real dragon will fly out.*"

I like those words. I remember them while I lie in the dark and the quiet, there on the hard floor.

The words give me an idea.

CHAPTER 5

Real Dragons

I whisper my idea to Tuyet and she agrees to help me. A week later, she has managed to collect everything I need from the cotton factory to make my idea a reality. I was scared Tuyet's hand would heal before she could gather it all.

Every day, she has been on all fours picking up the cotton fabric offcuts for dumping, like a dog sniffing around for food. But Tuyet hasn't dumped the biggest bits of cotton – she's managed to wrap them around her body under her shirt and smuggle them back here.

The fabric scraps are all white. White can mean purity, but it also means death, and that feels unlucky. So I stole some red thread from the reel on the sewing machine because red is the luckiest colour. Then I borrowed Kim-Ly's big needle and started stitching the scraps together at night. I hid my work under a broken floorboard at the back of the dorm.

At first I told the other girls I was making myself an *ao dai* – a long, traditional dress. They all wanted to know why. Did I think I was going on a date with one of the sandblasting boys? They laughed.

"Is it Giang?" Kim-Ly said. "We've seen him looking at you."

I didn't even know who Giang was.

The next day I found the fabric all ripped apart. I said nothing. I just started to sew it together again at bedtime.

But then one of the girls, I don't know who, spread a rumour that I was making the dress for Yen so she would be nice to me. Someone else said I was making the dress for one of the bosses to get extra food for myself. Some of the girls grabbed me after lights out and shook me upside down, like they thought food would fall from me. Tuyet punched one of them with her good hand and threatened the others, but they only backed down when they realised I had nothing to take.

The only way to stop the attacks was to share my idea.

I'm trying to make a sign. A banner, almost five metres long. If we can force the high windows open, we can hang it outside. It will run from one windowsill to the other, three storeys up. Hopefully people in the office building across the parking lot will see it.

"What will the sign say?" Chau asks me.

"Duh! It'll say 'Chau is a chicken brain'," says Tuyet, then coughs loudly. "What do you think it'll say? 'Help us!'"

"I'll write, 'Slaves here'," I tell her. "'Please call police.'"

Chau stares and asks, "Can you really spell all that?"

"I think so." I nod. "Yes, I can." I want Chau to feel hope, like I do.

"How will you get it to stay up out there?" Kim-Ly wants to know.

"We need someone tall who can reach the window," I say. "Someone to secure the banner edges just over the top of the windowsill. Then, when the windows are closed, they'll trap some of the fabric and hold it in place."

Kim-Ly raises an eyebrow. "I'm tallest," she says.

"Will you do it?" I ask her. "If we can fix it in place, someone's bound to see it."

"Yeah," Ping pipes up. "One of the bosses will see it from their Mercedes in the parking lot. And they'll punish us real bad. *All* of us."

"Don't worry," I mutter. "I'll say it was my idea."

"Screw that," Tuyet says with a grin and a wink. "I'll say it was *your* idea, Ping."

Ping scowls. "Be serious," she says.

"Yeah, like Ping could ever have an idea," Kim-Ly teases.

"I mean it," says Ping. "What's going to happen to us if no one calls the police and the bosses catch us?"

Chau's voice is only little, but it somehow fills the room: "What's going to happen to us if we don't even try?" she says.

Her words seem to hang in the stale air.

"If we can force the windows open," Kim-Ly says, "I think your idea could work, Hanh."

My cheeks flush with pride. I try to act like I never had a doubt.

"If it *doesn't* work," says Tuyet, "at least we'll let some fresh air in here."

Ping nods reluctantly. "But the nails in the window frames must be really long," she says. "How do we get them out?"

I look to Kim-Ly. "Do you still have that needle?" I ask, and smile as she pulls it from her waistband. "We can bend the needle into a hook and sort of work it under the head of the nail. That way we can try to pull the nail loose ..."

It feels good to plan. To work for ourselves. For the first time since I got here, I don't want to sleep. I want to act right now. I feel strong. Powerful. Vengeful.

I'm like the dragon ready to fly loose from its prison.

*

Of course, no one learns to fly in a moment.

We have to be careful. Especially with that boy in the Room – Giang. The one that Kim-Ly reckons was looking at me. He doesn't say much while he blasts sand at the denim, but I

have the feeling he listens a lot. His dark eyes
do often swing my way, but still I manage to
steal more thread to hold our banner together.

That's not all. In the courtyard, I find a stick that I snap to give it a sharp edge – this will be my pen.

Chau and Ping scoop black mud from the waste ground by the fence. When I mix it with water, this will be my ink.

I try to get two letters drawn each night. I don't have long to work before the lights go out, and it's difficult to get the mud to stain the cotton clearly. I have to draw the letters over and over to make the dark colour strong enough. I hope I'm spelling the words correctly.

SLAVES HERE. CALL POLICE.

I feel bad for not saying "please". But without it the message can be bigger and I can finish it faster.

My fellow slaves are growing excited. The Tày girls sit in front of the door, blocking it while I'm working. That way, if Yen bursts in, they can cause a commotion and give me time to fold up the banner and hide it under the floorboard.

Chau helps me write faster by preparing other sticks with the mud-ink mix. As one stick runs out, she passes me another and then loads up the first stick for when the second runs dry.

Meanwhile, Kim-Ly and Tuyet have been working together with the long, bent needle to wiggle out the nails hammered down through the bottom rails of the windows into the outside sill. After a couple of nights, their fingertips started to bleed. If Yen noticed, she'd be suspicious. So now they've organised a rota – different pairs of girls working to loosen the nails, just for a few minutes each night. That way each team coming to it is strong and fresh.

And determined.

When the final nail comes free at last, we stare at each other like no one can believe it.

"Wonder when these windows were opened last?" I whisper.

Tuyet stands up on her tiptoes. She turns the stiff window catch, puts her good hand to the dusty wood and shoves. The window jumps open with a splintering sound.

People gasp. Led by Chau, there's a sudden stampede to breathe the air that blows in. The sound of their footsteps seems too loud. What if the bosses come to investigate?

I push people away and rush to shut the window again. But the wood has warped over time and it won't fit back in its frame. I swear and I beg my ancestors for help like I've seen Ma and Grandma do.

And suddenly, with a scrunching sound, it closes again.

"Smooth," Tuyet mutters, her voice full of sarcasm.

We abandon the window and join everyone else on the floor. I'm shaking, terrified that someone is going to come and find out what we've been doing. But the corridor outside stays quiet.

I feel dizzy with fear, but I have to carry on. I use my last bathroom break to soak toilet water into some rags. I also use one of the writing sticks to scrape grime from between the damp tiles to make a thicker ink.

I open the door and surprise Ping, who is waiting just outside in the corridor. She looks up at me and I see a light stirring in her dark eyes. "Is it ready?" she asks.

I nod. "I'll finish it tonight," I whisper.

Ping gasps. "Then we put up the sign tomorrow morning?"

"Quiet," I hiss, and nod again. "Just before our shift. It has to be then."

Ping bites her lip and hugs herself and goes into the bathroom. I hear a noise from the staircase. I turn and find Yen staring at me from the end of the landing. There's a boy behind her in the shadows. I can't see who. He walks up the stairs, back to the male dorm.

Yen pushes out her chin and says, "What you looking at, baby?"

I turn away and hurry back into our dorm. I lie down, waiting until the last girl has taken her turn in the bathroom and Yen turns the big key in the lock. No more disturbances.

I unfold the banner, working before my "ink" can dry on the stick. The faintest moonlight shines through scuffs in the dirty glass. I fill the outline of the last letter on the sign to a soundtrack of Tuyet's hoarse breathing and the whispers of the other girls.

It's hard to see. Slowly the whispers stop and the snoring starts, and Ping turns and twists beside Tuyet.

I fall asleep hunched over with my hair scattered across the fabric. When I wake, faint grey light is stirring outside. My legs have pins and needles and my neck aches, but I rub my eyes and study the thick strokes on the banner.

Chau is sitting up looking at me. Her eyes are bright. "When do we hang it?" she whispers.

I take a deep breath. "Now," I say.

CHAPTER 6

"This is on you"

Tuyet has one of her coughing fits, but she's using it to get everyone's attention – so they know: *we're doing this.* Tuyet signals to the Tày girls to block the door and nods at Kim-Ly. Kim-Ly crosses to the window and pulls out the loosened nails. She passes each one to Ping, who looks sick. Meanwhile, Chau helps me stretch out the banner to its full width. The black ink strokes pop in contrast to the white. They'll be our voice.

And that's good because I've lost my own voice below the thumping heartbeats that rise through my chest. I think this is the best time to hang the sign because the people who work in the office opposite our window will surely be arriving soon. They'll see our work. Maybe most will think it is a joke, a prank. They might ignore it. But it only takes one person to call the police.

Surely one person will believe us?

It sounds all quiet outside on the landing. I decide we're safe to move. Kim-Ly helps me open the noisy window. After what happened last time, we both fake a coughing fit to cover the sound. On tiptoes, I peer through the open window. The courtyard three storeys below is deserted. Kim-Ly takes one end of the banner and leans out of the window with it in her hands. She starts trying to tuck the top edge into the gap between the window and its frame.

"Wait," I hiss, "the banner's upside down!"

Kim-Ly looks embarrassed. I forget I'm the only one who can read. She leans out dangerously, trying to fold it over to read the right way around. "Be careful," I hiss at her as she feeds the fabric through to me.

"Ping," Tuyet says, "help me open the other window."

But Ping is backing away, shaking her head. "No," she whispers. "No, we're gonna get caught. They'll never let us go home if we do this."

"You think they will anyway?" Tuyet hisses. "Come on."

Chau looks scared too but determined. "I'll try," she says. She reaches up, twists the catch and pushes at the window. It's jammed solid. Tuyet runs the needle up and down the frame where it opens, trying to prise out whatever's making it stick. Chau pushes against the dirty glass but it cracks, like a shard of lightning in the window pane.

My eyes scream "NO!" at her. How do we hide that? Yen will see it in a glance.

Tuyet knows what I'm thinking as she forces the window open at last. "It's OK," she says. "We'll smear more dirt on the crack to cover it."

Kim-Ly is still leaning through the right-hand window, with the other end of the banner in her hand. She needs to pass it to Tuyet, who is trying to reach out of the window on the left. Kim-Ly tosses the fabric across the gap between them. Tuyet lunges for it, but she misses. The end of the banner flaps down towards the stinking rubbish far below. I grip the other end of the fabric for dear life. If we lose the banner now, we've lost everything.

Kim-Ly reels in the banner to try again and Chau gets a push from Tuyet. Once she's scrambled up the wall to the window, Chau kneels on the sill. Tuyet holds tight on to her legs so Chau can lean out of the window to grab the other end of the banner. Kim-Ly throws it across and Chau catches it. She smiles at me, proudly.

Then I hear the sound of the key turning in the lock. Did I miss Yen's footsteps and the warning rattle? The door is kicked open and

slams into the Tày girls. One screams, falling forward as an angry man boots her aside. Two more men come in behind him. They're coming for us.

I back away from the window and the first man pushes Kim-Ly into me. We fall against the wall. The second man grabs a handful of Tuyet's hair and yanks her head back. She cries out and loses her grip on Chau. The third

man lunges for Chau's legs. She's still clutching the banner as she crawls out onto the narrow ledge outside the window and tries to stand.

I realise Chau is trying to hold up the banner herself, desperate for anyone out there to see it. But now my end of the banner comes loose from the window as she pulls up on it. Chau twists on the ledge, losing her balance.

Kim-Ly hides her face, but I can't.

It's the longest second of my life. Chau looks back into the dorm. I see panic in her big dark eyes.

She's already falling.

Chau's scream seems almost an afterthought. A loud, wet thump from down below cuts it off. I run to the window and stare down, numb. Chau's twisted body lies like a small island in a sea of black bin bags. The banner covers her face and torso, hiding her from sight.

I turn angrily to the men. "Get down there and help Chau," I say. "Take her to hospital!"

"Please," Tuyet groans, her head still being pulled back by one of the men.

He nods wearily to the first man. "Go out and clean it up," he says.

"*It?*" I say. I can't believe what I'm hearing. "*Chau* has fallen. *She* needs—"

He cuffs me round the face with the side of his hand, hard enough to knock me to my knees. "This is on you!" he bellows.

The words ring in my ears and stifle my voice. I can't speak. I can barely breathe.

"You will start work now!" the man shouts at our eleven silent faces. "No bathroom breaks. No food. You'll start *now*."

*

The day passes in a grey blur. The sewing machine spits out its stitches, but I feel like the machine's controlling me, not the other way around.

No one has told us a thing about Chau.

We've just been left here to stew. Yen's not in the Room to boss us around, but we're working even harder than normal. As if we can prevent the punishment that we know must be coming.

I don't think once about the food we're missing. I'd be sick if I tried to eat it anyway. I keep seeing Chau in my mind, her body like a dumpling floating in the dark broth of bin bags. And the words that started this ring out in my head – Uncle Ho's poem. The prison door was open just for a moment, but there was no dragon to fly out. Only a friend who fell.

Guilt and shame turn my stomach. I know it was an accident, but I also know ...

It's all my fault.

Kim-Ly sits neatly folded in her chair beside me, focused on her sewing. She's grinding her teeth the whole time. I can't look at her. I can't look at anyone. I hate that my idea didn't work. I hate myself for what I helped to happen, and I hate *them* for driving me to it.

And I find something is nagging at the back of my mind.

How did they know?

It wasn't just bad luck that Yen's wake-up call was delivered by three men this morning, each ready for trouble. They sneaked up to surprise us. They knew what we were planning to do and when we were planning to do it.

Someone told.

I turn to look at Ping, working her sanding tool over a denim cuff. I remember our talk on the landing outside the bathroom. Yen staring from the other end of the landing. She couldn't have heard, could she? She'd have done something about it there and then.

But I remember how Ping backed away from the window and said she wanted no part of what we were trying to do.

Did Ping rat on us?

Ping must sense my eyes on her. She glances up at me, then back down at what she's doing.

Just then the door flies open. Yen bursts in like a missile and I'm her target. She explodes on contact, lifting me from my chair in a headlock. Yen slams me head-first into the big steam press and my vision sparks into dizzy blackness. I fall to my knees.

"I know that sign was your idea," Yen snarls. "You're the only one who can write."

The steam-press lid swings open and I hear a thick and furious hiss.

"Well, you won't be writing again," Yen growls. "Not ever." She hauls me up and thrusts my bare right arm down on the board. I'm too shocked to even struggle.

When Yen brings down the press, I know that the scalding heat will burn the flesh from my bones.

CHAPTER 7

Breaking Down

"You thought you were so clever, didn't you, pig?" Yen rasps in my ear. "Well, this is where being clever gets you."

As my sight returns, I see the steaming press, ready to slam down on my wrist. And I see red marks on Yen's forearm. Six of them, raised like long pursed lips. It looks like she's been caned. Like I said, she dishes punishments out, but she has to take them too. Because of us.

"You don't want to do this," I cry. "Think. How do I turn out 150 pairs of embroidered jeans a day with one arm?"

Yen is panting with anger. But the lid of the press stays where it is.

"How many times will they cane you when we don't make the quotas?" I say, struggling up and pulling my arm away.

Yen scowls but doesn't move to stop me.

Suddenly, despite everything, I feel like I've got the upper hand. We're kept here to work. We'll only work more slowly if the bosses starve us further, or hurt us more, or cage us up for longer. And in the long run, that will hurt them maybe even more than us. We are already at rock bottom – where else is there to take us?

"You need me," I tell Yen, and my voice sounds calm and strong. "You can't hurt me."

"Maybe you're right, Hanh," Yen says, her face twisting in a leer. "But if you cause any more trouble, I *won't* hurt you. I'll hurt Tuyet."

I flinch. Yen sees it.

"I'll make that hole in her hand look like an insect bite," Yen goes on. "And don't worry about Tuyet not being able to work. We have plenty of jobs a cripple can do. If Chau ever wakes up, you can ask her all about it."

The sudden hope inside me burns harder than the steam press ever could. "Chau's alive?" I ask.

"Shouldn't think she has enough brains left to string a sentence together," Yen replies.

I know Yen's trying to be cruel, but all I can feel is relief. "Chau *is* alive," I say.

"You call that living?" Yen sneers.

"You call *this* living?" I say. Then I turn and retreat to my seat. I fire up the sewing machine. I start on the next pair of jeans. I don't want anything worse to happen to Tuyet. And I want Chau to get better. I won't make more waves. I'll be good, respectful Hanh. Hanh, whose name means "right behaviour".

I take a deep breath. Wipe my eyes.

Work.

*

After all that, the days pass in a blur of work. I feel like I've become a robot. I even talk to the sewing machine in my head, like I used to talk to the chickens in our yard. I don't dare think about happier times, because if I do, I'm not sure I'll be able to go on. And I have to. I have to keep working as one mountain of jeans is taken away and another is dumped beside me. I'm pulling my weight. Sucking up the tiredness, the boredom. The din and the stink.

I can't let anyone else be hurt.

Tuyet is back in the Room. Her hand is OK, but her breathing is worse. She's had to breathe in lungfuls of cotton fluff and traffic fumes from her cross-city trips to the other factory. Not much better than the sand in here, I guess.

Having Tuyet back makes me nervous. Yen comes in and stands behind Tuyet at the press. Just stands there. Threatening. Trying to get to me.

"When we leave here, I'm gonna split Yen's jaw," Tuyet tells me gruffly, late one night in the dark.

I don't answer. I'm staring at our boarded-up windows. I remember the little bits of light that snuck in past the dirt, and the patterns they made.

"Hanh?" Tuyet says. Her hand touches my back. "It's OK. We *will* get out of here."

The little bits of light at the windows were like stitches. I used to twist them into shapes in my mind. Water buffalo. Bison.

Dragons.

Tuyet leans in closer and says, "Hanh, I know you're awake."

If she does, it's more than I know.

*

One morning I come out of the bathroom and Ping's there, ghostly in the gloom.

"It wasn't me," she says.

I try to push past her, but she blocks my way.

"I know you must think it was me who ratted," Ping says. "But I didn't. I'm pretty sure it was Giang – the sandblaster boy. The one who watches and listens."

I shrug.

"See, in the Room I heard a boy say that Giang got better food than they did the night after we got caught," Ping goes on. "And the boys' dorm is upstairs. Giang could have come down and heard us talking here."

I remember the shadow of the boy I saw behind Yen on the landing. It might have been Giang. But if he'd overheard us, he'd have told Yen about our plans right there and then. Wouldn't he? But Yen didn't know. She was caned by the bosses for not knowing.

My head aches. "It doesn't matter," I say.

Ping looks sadder and lowers her voice. "Did you hear any more about Chau?"

"No," I say. Again I try to push past.

Ping grabs my arm. "What if I stitch extra labels in the clothes, labels that say HELP?" she says. "That could work, right? Can you spell HELP for me?"

I close my eyes. *Don't be stupid*, I want to shout. Even if we knew the address of this place – even if we could write a thousand labels – these clothes are sold all over the world. Our language would mean nothing to the people who buy the things we make. Just like *we* mean nothing to them.

But Ping still has hope. For a spiteful moment, I want to stamp her hope out and leave her feeling the same as me. But I don't. I bite my tongue.

"It's too risky to try again," I tell her. And I go back to the dorm and I wonder where Chau is now.

*

Several days pass and then the sandblasting machine breaks down. This is a really big deal. The machine is the fastest way to wear down the denim – the bosses won't meet their quotas if it's all done by hand. And if they don't deliver on time, they might lose orders.

The sandblaster sometimes clogs up or strips a gear or something, and when it does, the handyman at the factory fixes it. But this time the machine has really gone wrong. Two repairmen come in from the world outside. They wear cream overalls with a red logo that says FIX IT HANOI. Do they know we're all slaves here? I wonder what would happen if I begged them for help. What would they do?

But I don't get a chance to open my mouth. Yen is watching all of us like a hawk.

One of the repairmen turns to her. "We heard someone broke the machine on purpose," he says. "You got enemies out there?"

Yen's eyes flash, like she's furious he's said anything at all. "We think someone tried to break in last night," she admits.

"I think you'll find they *did* break in," the man says with a smile. "There's water and gravel in the motor."

There's a low buzz through the Room. Someone broke into the factory and messed up the sandblaster? Why?

It's like Yen knows what we're thinking. "Security has been ramped up," she tells the repairman, loud enough for everyone to hear. "No one will be sneaking in or out again. Now, how long till you get it working?"

"We'll clean it out as best we can," says the repairman. "But you really need a new machine."

I wish the old machine would blow up in the repairmen's faces. Let the bosses go broke buying a new machine. But I know it would make no difference to us. They'd just move us to other factories like the one Tuyet was sent to.

The other repairman is hardly working. He hasn't spoken. He's just staring at Tuyet. Creep. Then he looks round and his eyes fix on me. No one else. Just me.

Looking away, I get on with my work. I let my thoughts go. But it feels as if my daydreams are being stabbed by the busy needle of the sewing machine and ground between Kim-Ly's teeth.

*

A couple of hours later, the sandblaster is working again. Whoever broke in here didn't do much. The repairmen fire the high-pressure sand at the wall and floor and laugh as it sprays out like smoke. Like it's a game they're playing. They only stop when Tuyet bends over in a coughing fit.

"You need masks when you're working this thing," says the chatty repairman. He holds out some paperwork for Yen to sign.

Yen pushes it away. "I don't deal with this," she says. But the man says he only needs a signature, any signature. Yen looks embarrassed. I suppose she's better with a stick than a pen.

The repairman's friend has been slowly heading for the door. Now he stops in front of me. He has a stick of gum in his hand. For a moment, I think he's going to offer the gum to me. My mouth waters. He unwraps the gum and puts it in his mouth, chewing with relish to let me know how good it tastes. Then he balls up the silver paper and throws it at me. It bounces off my cheek and onto the desk.

"Read," he whispers to me. Then the other repairman joins him, waves the signed sheet of paper and leads the way out of the Room.

My fingers work without my brain, unwrapping the ball of paper.

There's tiny writing inside the wrapper. I squint.

HELP COMING IN FIVE DAYS. BLOCK DORM DOOR AT LIGHTS OUT TO STAY SAFE.

It's as if my heart stops.

Then I catch movement. Yen is like a dark bullet firing towards me. I push the paper into my mouth and chew fast.

"What's that?" Yen demands. "What did he give you?"

"He threw his gum wrapper in my face," I tell her. And as I swallow, I shrug. "It still tastes like gum."

I see the suspicion on Yen's face turn to disgust. Maybe, just for a moment, something like pity. She turns around and stalks over to hassle the Tày girls. I feel the wad of chewed paper in my gut and close my eyes, memorising every word.

When I open them, I see Giang starting up the sandblaster again. He looks across at me. He smiles. He has a nice smile.

I look away, stare down at my work and act like nothing's happened. But now the rattling of the needle sounds different.

I'm not sure if it sounds like urgent encouragement in my ears. Or like lies and laughter.

CHAPTER 8

Voices in the Dark

I don't sleep so well. My belly aches and I begin to wonder if I imagined the message on the paper.

But I remember the words between Yen and the repairman:

"We think someone tried to break in last night."

"Someone broke the machine on purpose."

And this gets me thinking.

What if the repairmen sneaked into the Room and broke the sandblaster in the night – knowing they would be called in to fix it? Not just to make money for themselves, but to see what was happening inside? To pass me that message?

Get over yourself, says a voice in my head. *What's so special about you?*

"Because I can read as well as write," I say out loud. Maybe Ma and Dad have been looking for me. Maybe they told the police in Hanoi and *they're* looking ...

Should I tell anyone? A part of me wants to say nothing. It's all too fantastic. The note in the gum wrapper could just be a cruel trick that the repairman played on me. It's got to be.

But hope isn't so easily put out. And as hope grows in me, it feels more dangerous. I saw the hope in Ping's eyes when she was still trying to think up ways to escape. I hear it in Tuyet's voice when she dreams of finally standing up to Yen and getting her revenge.

*

A day goes by and I say nothing about the message on the chewing-gum wrapper. It's as if saying it out loud will jinx it – if it's even real. But just imagine it *is* real and no one is ready when help comes. It would be my fault all over again.

Why couldn't that man have thrown his gum wrapper at someone else?

I'm still thinking about it the next night while we're out shuffling round the courtyard in the moonlight.

I hear voices shouting behind the wall, in the parking lot. Angry, threatening voices warning someone away. The mortar between the breeze blocks has crumbled in places and I can just see through.

I see Gum-Paper Man facing up to three guys. One of them shoves him against a car. He rolls over the bonnet to put the car between him and them. Gum-Paper Man looks scared. His eye is swollen and bruised.

"I'm sorry, OK?" he says. "I left some tools here when we fixed the machine, so I just came back to get them. I didn't want to bother your bosses ..."

I guess the guys that Gum-Paper Man is talking to don't believe his story. One of them throws a brick at him, but Gum-Paper Man ducks. The brick bashes the car roof and sets off the alarm. Lights flash and a siren wails. Gum-Paper Man turns and runs. The three men tear after him.

Then I'm shoved away by others longing to look. Anything out of the ordinary is like an oasis in the desert of our days. I drift from the crowd, feeling sick.

Gum-Paper Man said help was coming.
Why was he back here again? Have the bosses
learned of his plan, so now it's all off? Did
someone see him throw the message at me?

I close my eyes, too weary even to cry.
What was I thinking, daring to hope that help
could come?

The woman who watches us in the
courtyard steps out from the doorway, shouting
and shooing at us like we're chickens, telling us
to go back inside. Everyone seems stirred up.
I'm closest to the door, so I go inside first. My
head's in a total daze.

*

That night I share everything with Tuyet. She
can't believe it, gripping my fingers in the dark,
trembling with excitement.

"The Gum-Paper Man might have got away from those other guys," Tuyet whispers. "The bosses might not know anything about the message he gave you."

"Sure," I whisper.

"He said help was coming, right? That means he's not acting on his own." Tuyet pauses. "Hey, maybe Chau's all right and she told the police!"

"It's all *maybe*, *might*, *could be*," I say and sigh. "We don't *know* anything!"

Tuyet says, "Well, three nights from now, if help comes, we will know."

"What do we do in the meantime?" I whisper.

"We keep quiet, Hanh," Tuyet says. "Until the night it's meant to happen. Then we can all lie in front of the door to block it. All of us."

I think about that. "Yeah, that could work," I whisper. "All of us together – we'd make a pretty good barricade."

Tuyet nods. "There's plenty of dead wood in here, for sure."

We laugh softly. A part of me wants to believe we will get out of here. A soft, secret part of the old Hanh that's somehow clung on all this time. This part of me is crouched in the dark, considering its chances.

Can help really be coming? I stare up at the boarded windows and wonder.

*

Two more exhausting days pass. Bulbs like eyeballs in the ceiling glare down while we work our long shift until it's lights out in the dorm again. The darkness slips like a sack over our heads. Our lullaby is the sound of the key as it rattles and jangles in the lock.

Minutes tick past in the darkness. And then the uneasy silence explodes with the sound of voices outside on the landing. Furious, shouting voices.

"They're coming!" someone yells just outside the door.

What? In a heartbeat, all my senses are on high alert. Help can't be coming now – can it? It's a night too soon.

"Get this lot down into the minibus," a man says. "Move them to the Dai Tu warehouse."

The other girls are whispering, afraid. I hear Kim-Ly close by call out, "What's happening?"

Plans have changed, I realise. *Gum-Paper Man – he must have sneaked back here to try to warn me, but they stopped him before he could. He's on his way tonight!*

"Everyone get up," I shout. "Come on, up! We have to block the door."

Kim-Ly groans. "What are you talking about?"

There's no time to explain. No time to do anything. Footsteps thump up to the door and the key turns. Light from outside breaks into the blackness. Silhouetted figures burst into the dorm.

"Don't let them take you!" I shout to the other girls. "Help is coming. The bosses want to take us away before it gets here ..."

But the men are shouting me down and some of the girls are screaming. I see Ping dragged from the dorm with two other girls and pushed out onto the landing. Ping screams as she's thrown face down onto the floorboards.

Our chance to escape is over before it's even begun.

CHAPTER 9

Broken Threads

I'm too numb to struggle as a woman drags me from the dorm and forces me to my knees. Someone's got a clipboard, ticking each of us off on a list to make sure no one's missing. I look across the landing and see the boys being taken downstairs, shouted at and hit with sticks when they answer back.

Tuyet is coughing her lungs up beside me. One of the men kicks her hip, then waves the baton in his hand and says she'll get more if she doesn't shut up.

In that moment, I know: *if we don't make this stop tonight, it will never stop.*

And before I can even think, I throw myself at the man who kicked Tuyet and knock him backwards. He yelps in surprise, loses his balance and falls into the bathroom. His baton falls from his fingers. I swing the door shut, hoping to trap him inside. But the door bites into his ankle instead.

The man yells. I hesitate. Then I slam the door on his leg again.

One of the other men grabs me by the back of my neck and raises his baton to strike me down. But I'm wild now. With a shout, I push him into the woman who grabbed me before. They both go down hard on the floorboards. But they're strong and well fed, and I am not. Already I can feel their fingers clamping down on my wrists, twisting and pulling, forcing me down.

But then there's a *CRACK* and the woman crumples limply to the floor. Kim-Ly stands over me, holding the first man's baton in her trembling hands. The second man tries to get up, but Kim-Ly plants her bare foot in the middle of his face and stamps him down. The back of his head slams into the floorboards and he's left senseless.

The adults who were steering the boys down the stairs have come running back up at the sound of the commotion.

"Everyone, *run!*" I yell. "They can't stop all of us!"

But they have a good try. A man grabs Kim-Ly, twists her long arms behind her back and slams her cheek to the wall. Her scream cuts through me. Ping tries to duck between the legs of the woman blocking her way, but the woman catches Ping by the hair.

I dodge the arms that clutch for me and somehow I reach the stairs. I'm scared for my friends, but I know that help is close by. If we can just get out!

Tuyet is ahead of me, running down the stairs. "Come on!" she shouts as she makes it to the hall, gasping and wheezing. "Hanh ...?"

She stops and looks back at me. I see what Tuyet doesn't. It's Giang, looming from the shadows. Giang grabs hold of Tuyet's arm and pulls her into the Room.

"No!" I shout as the door swings closed behind them. I fly down the rest of the steps and charge after them.

I throw open the door and burst into the Room, but a leg pushes out in front of me. I trip. My palms sting as they scrape on the concrete floor and I gasp, winded.

Giang has Tuyet against the wall, her arm twisted up behind her back. "In here!" he yells. He's trying to attract the attention of the adults, but no one comes. Everyone else must still be up on the noisy landing.

"Get up and don't try anything," Giang hisses to me. "I don't want to hurt her, but I will."

"He must be the one that ratted on us about the banner," Tuyet gasps. "Got Chau nearly killed just to fill his belly."

"I had to," Giang says, and points to the sandblaster. "There's dust in my lungs, see? I'm sick. The bosses said it'll kill me if I don't get help."

"And they said they'd help you if you spy for them?" I say, and keep on staring. "You believed them?"

That's when Tuyet screams and twists her arm free of Giang's grip. Her fist cracks into his cheek and he falls backwards. Then Tuyet is leaning over me, hand held out, helping me up. Hope explodes in me like fireworks. If we can just get outside ...

But my fireworks go out as Yen strides into the Room and closes the door behind her. I see the red-stained baton in her hand. Tuyet recoils from it automatically. Giang grabs Tuyet by the shoulders.

Yen's eyes are dark as she says, "Hey, babies. Quite the party in here."

I think of the graffiti scrawled above the door: *One way in, no way out.* It mustn't be true! Desperate, I try to push past Yen, but she blocks my way and propels me backwards. I crash into my sewing machine.

"You know what, Hanh? I knew about your banner all along," Yen says. "I used to pull it out from under the floorboards each day while you were on shift to see how far you'd got with it."

Tuyet stares. "What?" she says.

"Yeah. I turned a blind eye," Yen goes on. "I thought your idea might actually work and this place would get busted."

I take a shaky breath, still clinging to my machine. "Why would *you* want that?" I say.

"I was taken from my village just like you," Yen says. "But people stopped looking for me a long time ago." She walks slowly up to Tuyet. "When Giang told the bosses about the banner, they punished me for not keeping a closer watch on you." Yen raises her baton. "I promised them I'd do better in future."

"You've made up for it now," Giang says. "They'll reward you, Yen, like me. More food, no beatings." He smiles. Like I told you, Giang has a nice smile.

Yen swings the baton and leaves that smile in bits. Tuyet is knocked clear as Giang spits out blood and teeth and falls to the ground.

Yen swoops over Giang and holds the baton against his throat.

I stare at her. "Yen, what are you doing?"

"Leave me alone," Yen hisses. "Maybe you two can save yourselves. As for me ..."

She pushes down, throttling Giang.

"Don't!" I shout. "We can all get out of here ..."

But I'm already too late. A man is standing in the doorway. "Get away from that boy," he orders Yen. "Drop the baton."

Yen is distracted for a moment and I yank the baton from her hands. But I don't let go of it. Yen slowly steps away from Giang, who stays down, panting and groaning. I grip the stick, ready to fight.

"Wait," says Tuyet, talking to the man in the doorway. "I recognise you."

And in a flash I see that it's Gum-Paper Man. Not in overalls now but in a scruffy suit. He's got a bruise on his chin to match the one on his eye, and he's panting hard.

I stare at him. "Who are you?" I ask.

"A friend," he says. "Nearly got myself killed trying to get back into your building a couple of nights ago."

I flush as I realise: "You *were* trying to warn me!"

"I knew I was pushing my luck after I broke in to wreck the sandblaster," Gum-Paper Man admits. "We have a friend in the repair firm your bosses use and they got me on the job. But when I came back, your bosses checked and saw I wasn't on the payroll. They got suspicious."

"So that's why the bosses tried to move us all out tonight?" Yen says.

"That's right," Gum-Paper Man agrees. "Meant we had to move earlier than planned." He looks between Yen and Giang. "Just in time, huh?"

Again I ask him, "Who *are* you?"

Before he can answer, a woman strides in and places a hand on Gum-Paper Man's arm. "All right, I've got this," she says. "Help the police mop things up on the landing. See who you can identify."

Gum-Paper Man nods. "You got it." He gives me a warm smile. Then he leaves.

This woman looks smart – and not just her clothes. Her face. Her whole manner. "Hanh?" she asks, her voice low and calm. "I'm a care worker with a charity called Child Traffic. My name is Vu Lam Minh. Are you all right?"

I stare at the woman. I can't find words.

It's weird. I've wanted to shriek and howl to be let out ever since I arrived. I am here in the Room where the noise and dust and stink and the hours have torn holes in me like I'm made of denim. Now the big door that shut us in here stands open.

I thought I'd rise from my prison like a dragon: strong and noble, breathing fire at my enemies. Instead, I'm standing still and silent. And you know what? That peace feels powerful. There's no sand bursting from the hose. No chatter of needles or scalding steam or grinding of teeth. Only the stink of the dye and the sweat remains, like the memory of violence. Like Giang stirring on the floor.

"It's over now, Hanh," says Vu Lam Minh. "The police raid went well and no one is badly hurt. You're safe. We're going to get you home."

"Everyone?" says Tuyet.

"Even me?" Yen whispers.

"All of you," says Minh. She smiles at me as the baton finally falls from my fingers and clatters on the floor. "Everyone is going home."

CHAPTER 10

Paying the Price

I'm not sure if you can really call this a happy ending. But it's a lot happier than it could have been. Perhaps, sometimes, that's all we can ask for.

Cos things don't really end in real life, do they? There are always echoes. After-effects. Consequences.

I couldn't be more thankful that I made it out of Hanoi. But I still have nightmares. I still get teased at school for being older than the other kids in my class. And my dad looks so much older now. He feels so guilty after what happened – it's kind of broken him.

Dad never received another penny after the first bit of money the Man and the Woman gave him. He still asks forgiveness for letting me go to Hanoi. Not just from me but from Ma, from my sisters, from his ancestors ...

I've told Dad a hundred times that I don't blame him for what happened. Like I don't blame Yen for hitting us, or even Giang for ratting us out. The stuff that happened is down to the bosses at our sweatshop. The decisions they made.

I guess the bosses would argue that they are victims too. The big clothing companies want stuff made so cheaply that honestly run factories can hardly make a profit. And so, these factories pass parts of the job on to sweatshops like ours that don't have to do things legally. They use children. Immigrants. The poor and the desperate.

The businessman who ran our sweatshop and the cotton factory was fined for breaking child labour laws. That's all. It wasn't even a very big fine. Not enough to stop him setting up again somewhere else.

I lie awake on my sleeping mat at night now, safe in my room with my sisters, and I listen to the calls of the forest birds and insects. But the sounds of the sweatshop sneak into my ears from out of nowhere and drip into my dreams. I often dream I'm shopping for clothes and then the shop doors close on me and I'm taken away.

I really hate that dream.

*

After Vu Lam Minh took me home, I didn't see any of the other girls until a "press call" in Song Cong City. The Child Traffic charity asked us to talk about our experiences to raise awareness.

It was so good to see Tuyet. Kim-Ly was there. I didn't hear her grind her teeth once. Ping was there too – turns out she wears glasses. I didn't realise she couldn't see so well. Chau was with them in a wheelchair and we just hugged and hugged when we saw each other.

Minh had brought our banner along – she'd found it in the trash where it had fallen, abandoned. She held it up for the people from the TV news and the press. Chau was upset to see it.

But truth is, Chau's the only reason we were found by the charity at all.

The banner might have seemed like a prank to anyone in the office building opposite. But a child falling – that was real. Someone saw and called the police. A couple of police officers came, but they didn't look too closely.

Luckily, Child Traffic heard about Chau's fall and did some looking about of their own.

Minh told me that the bosses had paid some drunken back-street doctor to take Chau off their hands. They said they'd take her back if he could heal her well enough to work. If not, the doctor would have to get rid of her.

The doctor was glad to pass Chau on to Child Traffic, who got her proper care. The stuff Chau told them about how we were treated convinced the police to raid the sweatshop and get us out.

Chau's going to need a lot of operations on her back before she can walk normally again. But Child Traffic is determined to raise the money somehow. Minh is trying to get treatment for Tuyet's breathing problems too. But that leaves the charity less money to track down other missing children from our province and its neighbours.

Tuyet says she wants to raise her own money. She's learning to become a mechanic. Gum-Paper Man is helping to train her. Child

Traffic have got Yen and Giang working for them too – they don't have homes to go to, so now they visit schools across northern Vietnam. Together they warn teachers and pupils about people like the Man and the Woman. Jackals on the lookout for hungry children from poor rural areas they can trick into slavery.

The more people learn about the slavers, the less successful they will be.

Minh asked me if I would speak about what I went through at the sweatshop, and that's why I've told my story to you. But I don't really like talking about it. I still think of the words above the door to the Room – *One way in, no way out*. For months, I was so sure that was true. But now I can see it was just one person's idea of the truth. We each have our own truths to find. But a lot depends on how hard we want to look.

When I look back, it's like seeing through prison bars. I want to look forward now. When I leave school, I want to become a fashion designer. I will start a business that treats workers fairly. We will not make cheap stuff that hurts people and the environment. And I want Chau to model my clothes.

"What if I never get out of this chair?" Chau says.

"You'll still model them," I tell her. "I promise."

We all need clothes. We all like to look good and feel comfortable. And clothes make a statement. They say something about who we are and the choices we make.

Next time you're shopping for clothes and you see that cute pair of ripped jeans and you just can't believe how little they cost ...

What will *you* choose?

Why I wanted to tell this story

The amount of clothes produced has more than doubled since the year 2000. Humans around the world are buying more clothes than ever. In total, the global fashion industry now produces around 80 billion pieces of clothing each year.

But while fashion has never been more affordable than today, it is costing the Earth. It takes more than 8,000 litres of water to make a single pair of jeans, from growing the cotton to washing and dyeing the fabric. That's almost as much as one person drinks in ten years. Making so many clothes produces 10 per cent of all greenhouse-gas emissions and 20 per cent of the world's waste water.

Big companies want to make as much money as they can, so they insist that the clothes they stock are made as cheaply as possible at every stage of production. As a result, the people who make these clothes are often paid very low wages – or not at all. They work in bad conditions. Sometimes they are treated as slaves, like Hanh and her friends in this book.

Experts believe that around 170 million children around the world are being forced into child labour. That's about 11 per cent of young people. Many of these make textiles and garments in atrocious conditions. Because they are working, they cannot go to school. And without qualifications they will be trapped in low-paid jobs as adults. That means that their own children's futures will be limited.

But it's not all bad news. Charities like the one in the story are real and helping to free child workers from illegal factories and giving them brighter futures. Many people in the textiles industry are also pushing for change. Some businesses are looking at creating clothes through recycling. This includes turning types of waste into clothing – even milk that has gone off!

There are other ways to take the pressure off the planet, such as cleaner recycling and fabrics that are more eco-friendly. But those who buy the clothes must change their behaviour too. We must learn to value our clothes and make better choices if we want to reduce the fashion industry's impact on the world.

One way to start is by asking questions about the brands you like. Find out if they use sustainable fabrics like organic cotton. Also consider spending more on well-made clothes that won't wear out so fast. Or care for and repair the clothes you own so they last longer. You can refresh your wardrobe by swapping clothes you don't need with your friends or siblings. You might also buy clothes from charity shops and cut down what you get from cheap fashion chains.

If children like Hanh could speak to you, they would ask for your help to make things better.

Will you help them?

Our books are tested
for children and young people by
children and young people.

Thanks to everyone who consulted on
a manuscript for their time and effort in
helping us to make our books better
for our readers.